Anthony Lewis Churchill
Illustrations by Shelley Eynon

Lucy the Triceratops Who Thinks She's a Fairy and that's Okay!

Bumblebee Books
London

A CIP catalogue record for this title is
available from the British Library.

ISBN: 978-1-83934-164-9

Bumblebee Books is an imprint of
Olympia Publishers.

First Published in 2021

Bumblebee Books
Tallis House
2 Tallis Street
London
EC4Y 0AB

Printed in Great Britain

www.olympiapublishers.com

Dedication

To all those who on my own journey have
helped me find my own 'Lucyness!'

In the beginning there was an egg!

At the turn of the 19th century, people lived in cities and in the country, some people in the country lived in big houses, such as this house, Ashton Court. It was the home of a very wealthy landowner called Sir Greville Smyth. He had a daughter Esme, whom he adored.

Greville loved to explore and travel the world. He would often bring back interesting things from his journeys. On one of these occasions, on a trip to the frozen forests of Canada he found an egg! Not just a normal egg from a chicken or a goose, but an enormous green speckled egg, from who knows where?

He brought the egg home and gave it to his beloved daughter Esme. She was a very shy and quiet little girl who did not have many friends. She kept the egg in her room by the side of her bed.

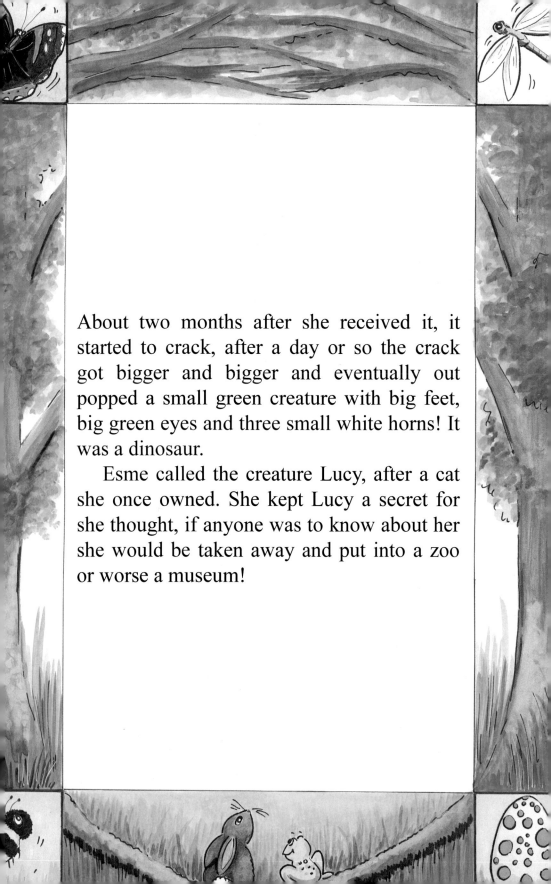

About two months after she received it, it started to crack, after a day or so the crack got bigger and bigger and eventually out popped a small green creature with big feet, big green eyes and three small white horns! It was a dinosaur.

Esme called the creature Lucy, after a cat she once owned. She kept Lucy a secret for she thought, if anyone was to know about her she would be taken away and put into a zoo or worse a museum!

The years went by and Esme and Lucy grew together, Esme grew faster than Lucy, for dinosaurs live a long time so they have more time to grow!

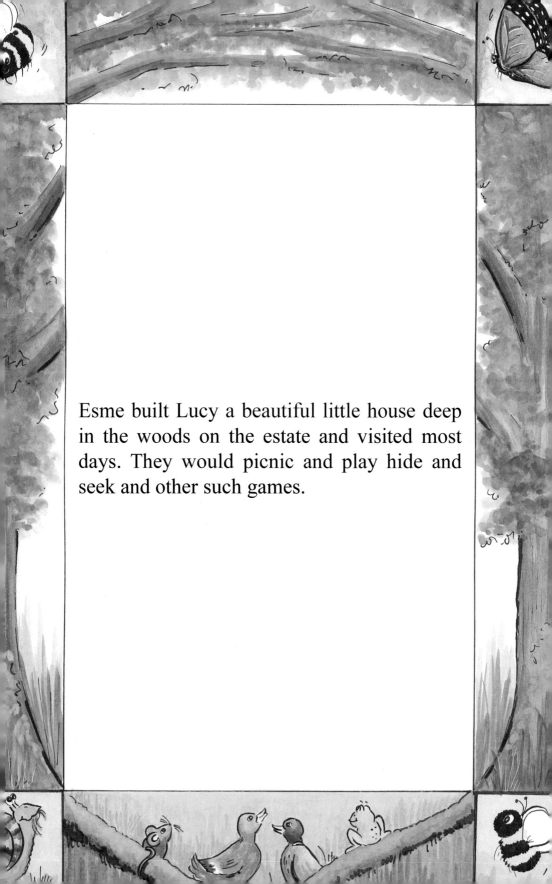

Esme built Lucy a beautiful little house deep in the woods on the estate and visited most days. They would picnic and play hide and seek and other such games.

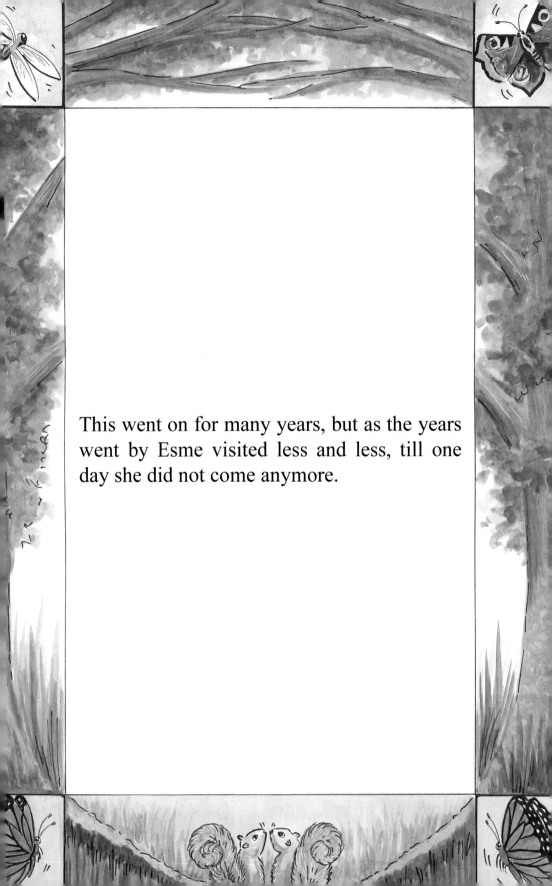

This went on for many years, but as the years went by Esme visited less and less, till one day she did not come anymore.

Lucy was sad but made friends with all the birds, bees, snails, flowers and trees so she did not get lonely. As the years went by, the estate was sold and Lucy never went near the house again, till now…

One day Lucy woke to the sound of her friends, the birds, and a very different sound of children playing nearby. Lucy lived deep in the woods so this was a new sound to her but reminded her of those days with Esme. She decided she would take a closer look. She hid behind a very big tree and peered out carefully so she would not frighten the child. It was a young girl, similar to Esme but wearing very different clothes.

All of a sudden the young girl noticed Lucy. She did not feel frightened and called out, "Hello there." Lucy stood back for a moment a bit unsure of whether to stay or run away. "Hello," said the young girl, "don't be afraid." Lucy stood very still has the young girl came closer towards her. The young girl reached out her hand and said, "Hi my name is Zoe, what's yours?" Lucy felt a warmth and kindness that she had not felt for such a long time, she moved out from behind the tree.

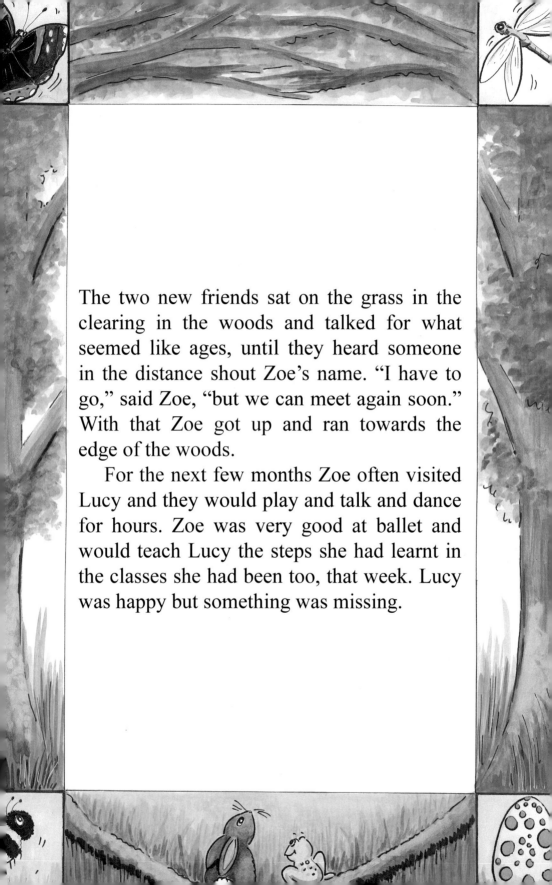

The two new friends sat on the grass in the clearing in the woods and talked for what seemed like ages, until they heard someone in the distance shout Zoe's name. "I have to go," said Zoe, "but we can meet again soon." With that Zoe got up and ran towards the edge of the woods.

For the next few months Zoe often visited Lucy and they would play and talk and dance for hours. Zoe was very good at ballet and would teach Lucy the steps she had learnt in the classes she had been too, that week. Lucy was happy but something was missing.

Lucy now had a dream, she dreamed of being a ballet dancer, she imagined what it must be like to be on the stage dancing to the beautiful music. One day Zoe came to visit and asked, "Lucy would you like to come and live with Me and my mum, in our house in the city?" Lucy said yes straight away, it was time for her to have a new adventure, she thought to herself.

Zoe lived with her mother who owned a flower shop in the city. When Lucy saw all the wonderful colours and smells of all the beautiful flowers she was very happy indeed. But there was one thing missing… she had always felt very much the odd one out, being a dinosaur, wouldn't you? After all, how many dinosaurs have you seen? There was no one to compare herself too! She started to ask questions and look through books but she never found the answer.

One day she looked in the mirror and said to herself, "I am unique, I am the only triceratops in the world and I love who I am."

Believing in yourself is so important and knowing who you are is so cool. Lucy would look into the mirror and love what she saw, her beautiful big eyes, wonderful smile, her green face and body, her big feet so she can walk faster and her small hands so she can pick delicate flowers and her wings, don't forget her wings! You must always find the good in you and not the bad. "Focus on all the beautiful things you have and you will radiate and shine so bright you will fill your world, and others around you with your amazing light," she says.

Lucy remembered back in the woods on the estate, she used to focus on her large nose and couldn't see beyond that! Until one day a passing snail told her that she was beautiful and unique. She started to believe in herself more and more until one day she looked at her reflection and agreed she was beautiful. She started to look at all the good things about her and her tiny, tiny wings started to grow, bigger and stronger.

These days she can fly higher than ever before, allowing her to have a better perspective on life! "When you look at the good things in your life and show gratitude for all you are, and that your life holds for you, your face lights up," she says with a big smile on her face.

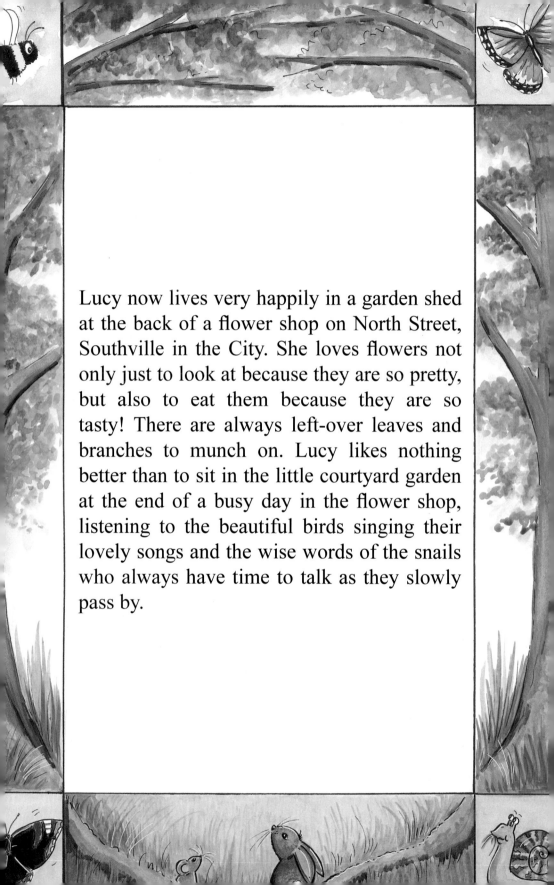

Lucy now lives very happily in a garden shed at the back of a flower shop on North Street, Southville in the City. She loves flowers not only just to look at because they are so pretty, but also to eat them because they are so tasty! There are always left-over leaves and branches to munch on. Lucy likes nothing better than to sit in the little courtyard garden at the end of a busy day in the flower shop, listening to the beautiful birds singing their lovely songs and the wise words of the snails who always have time to talk as they slowly pass by.

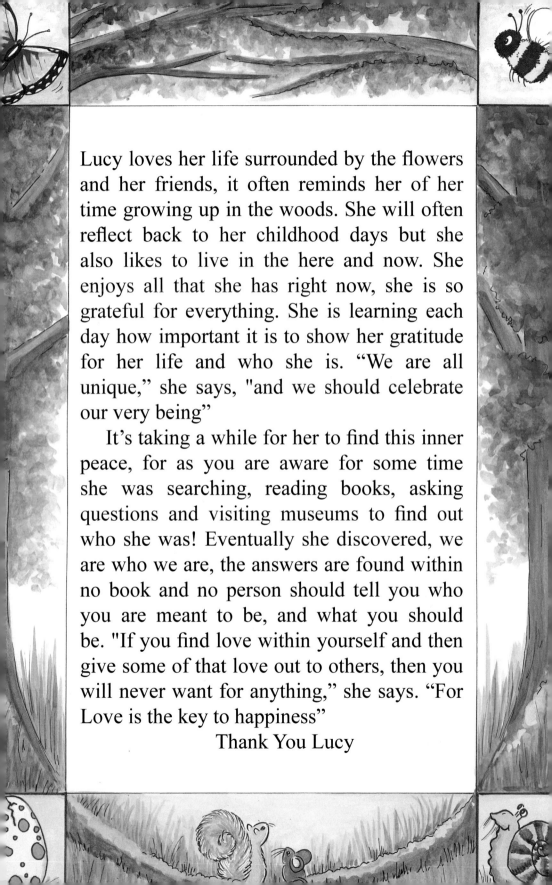

Lucy loves her life surrounded by the flowers and her friends, it often reminds her of her time growing up in the woods. She will often reflect back to her childhood days but she also likes to live in the here and now. She enjoys all that she has right now, she is so grateful for everything. She is learning each day how important it is to show her gratitude for her life and who she is. "We are all unique," she says, "and we should celebrate our very being"

It's taking a while for her to find this inner peace, for as you are aware for some time she was searching, reading books, asking questions and visiting museums to find out who she was! Eventually she discovered, we are who we are, the answers are found within no book and no person should tell you who you are meant to be, and what you should be. "If you find love within yourself and then give some of that love out to others, then you will never want for anything," she says. "For Love is the key to happiness"

Thank You Lucy

About the Author

Anthony Lewis Churchill, an artist, a writer, and a dream maker. Inspired by the world around him and the worlds beyond his eyes. He is an inventor and creator, combining reality and imagination. He was born in Bristol, a city in the United Kingdom where he spent his childhood, exploring, discovering and having great adventures and he dreamt of making this world a better place with his art and stories. He has spent his life bringing joy and happiness to thousands with his work, yet this is his first children's publication.

About the Illustrator

Started her creative journey in floristry and later honoured her artistic talents by illustrating and painting the flowers she used in her work. Upon having 4 children, she then began to paint pictures for them. This included characters that were based on her children, and the daft antics that they got up to. I like to create a painting that tells a story, often using days out with the family as inspiration.

Acknowledgements

Martin Williamson for his continued support